Sports Day

ILLUS... LEWIS

Everyone needs a team sticker. There you are!

Have you all got bottles of water? Keep your hats on.

I'm warming up. Which race are you in?

Which sticker do you have? Mine is pink!

You must try to run inside the white lines.

Lots of people have come to watch! Hi Dad!

Come back! You're not allowed on the race track!

We should have the baby in our team! She's so fast!

I'm better at jumping than running.

Run as fast as you can! Come on Red Team!

I'm out of breath! My legs are really tired.

I can see the finishing line. Faster!

The bean bag's got to land inside the hoop.

I'll have to throw it much harder next time.

Round the last cone. Am I faster than the others?

I hope I win. I'll collect some team points.

Come on, Yellow Team! Try and run faster!

Balancing this bean bag on my head is hard. Oops!

I've got a stopwatch. Let's see who gets the best time.

Run! Oh no! I've dropped it!

This hat is much too big for me. I can't see!

Buttons are hard to do!

This boot's too small for my foot. Heave!

Where are all these clothes from?

I've dropped my egg. Can I pick it up?

This egg's wobbling! Slow down! Careful!

Does it hurt? Don't worry. It's not too bad.

Do you want to rest, or run in the next race?

I love the obstacle race! I'm wobbling! Steady!

I think I can jump into the middle of the hoop!

I hope I win more team points. I'm in front!

It's hard to run and skip at the same time!

I'm running as fast as I can! Hand it to me!

Oh no! I've dropped the baton! Quick, pick it up!

Come on Pink Team! Nearly there! Faster!

The winner! First across the finishing line!

Hold onto the rope with both hands. Lean back!

When I blow the whistle – PULL! As hard as you can!

Pull the ribbon across the line. Harder!

I'm tired out! This is hard work! I keep on slipping.

How many teams are competing?

Which team has won the most points?

Hip hip hooray! Pink Team has won today!

Everyone's done really well.

We won! I can't wait until next year!

Hooray! Well done! Can I wave your flag?